AMERICAN ADVENTURES

★ ★ ★

THE BATTLES

The Revolutionary War
The War of 1812
The Civil War

Grateful acknowledgment is made to the following for permission to reprint previously published material:

The Scarlet Stockings Spy: A Revolutionary War Tale by Trinka Hakes Noble, illustrated by Robert Papp. Text copyright © 2004 by Trinka Hakes Noble. Illustrations copyright © 2004 by Robert Papp. Originally published by Sleeping Bear Press, 2004.

The Town that Fooled the British: A War of 1812 Story by Lisa Papp, illustrated by Robert Papp. Text copyright © 2011 by Lisa Papp. Illustrations copyright © 2011 by Robert Papp. Originally published by Sleeping Bear Press, 2011.

The Last Brother: A Civil War Tale by Trinka Hakes Noble, illustrated by Robert Papp. Text copyright © 2006 by Trinka Hakes Noble. Illustrations copyright © 2006 by Robert Papp. Originally published by Sleeping Bear Press, 2006.

—ɯᴚ—

Sleeping Bear Press™
315 E. Eisenhower Parkway, Ste. 200
Ann Arbor, MI 48108
www.sleepingbearpress.com

Printed and bound in the United States.

10 9 8 7 6 5 4 3 2 1

Library of Congress Cataloging-in-Publication Data • Noble, Trinka Hakes. • The battles / written by Trinka Hakes Noble, Lisa Papp; • illustrated by Robert Papp. • v. cm. – (American adventures) • Summary: "The Battles contains three stories focusing on key American battles. The Scarlet Stockings Spy is set in Philadelphia 1777 during the Revolutionary War. The Town that Fooled the British is set in Maryland during the War of 1812. The Last Brother is set on the battlefields of Gettysburg"– Provided by publisher. • Contents: The Scarlet Stockings spy — The town that fooled the British — The last brother. • ISBN 978-1-58536-861-7 • [1. Brothers and sisters–Fiction. 2. Gettysburg, Battle of, Gettysburg, Pa., 1863–Fiction. 3. Philadelphia (Pa.)–History–Revolution, 1775-1783–Fiction. 4. United States–History– Civil War, 1861-1865–Fiction. 5. Saint Michaels (Md.)–History–19th century–Fiction. 6. United States–History–War of 1812–Naval operations–Fiction.] • I. Papp, Lisa. II. Papp, Robert, illustrator. III. Title. • PZ7.N6715Bat 2013 • [Fic]–dc23 • 2012046805

TABLE OF CONTENTS

The Scarlet Stockings Spy

THE REVOLUTIONARY WAR

Trinka Hakes Noble

Illustrated by Robert Papp

In the fall of 1777, Philadelphia sat twitching like a nervous mouse. The British were going to attack, but no one knew where or when. Congress had fled inland to York. The Liberty Bell was hidden in Allentown. Folks thought the year resembled a hangman's gallows and took it as a bad sign. Now, all the church bells were being removed to keep the British from melting them down into firearms.

Uncertainty settled over the city like soot. Suspicions roamed through the cobblestone streets like hungry alley cats. Rumors multiplied like horseflies. Spies were everywhere.

Some spied for the British, loyal to the king. Others spied for the Patriots, loyal to Washington's army, now camped west of the city. Still other spies were loyal to lining their pockets.

But one little spy moved through the streets unnoticed, even though she wore scarlet stockings. Her name was Maddy Rose and she lived with her mother and brother in the Leather Apron District, next to the harbor, where the city's tradesfolk lived and worked in narrow brick row houses.

"Maddy Rose," called her mother from the front room, not looking up from her spinning. "Tarry not. Mistress Ross has need of these linens this morning."

Dusty eastern light filtered through the panes of thick glass in their tiny row house on Appletree Alley where the *click, clack, click* of the flax wheel never stopped from early dawn 'til candlelight.

"Yes, Mother," answered Maddy Rose, hurrying to poke up the fire.

Each morning, before she went to sew seams for Mistress Ross on Arch Street, Maddy Rose lowered the teakettle over the hearth, then crushed dried raspberry leaves to brew Liberty tea. Since the tea rebellion in Boston, drinking imported English tea was considered disloyal.

This morning her mother looked tired, so Maddy Rose added a drop of precious honey. Carefully she carried the only china teacup they owned to her mother, a treasured gift from her father.

"Here, Mother dear. This will refresh you."

Maddy Rose's mother stopped spinning and gently held her daughter's chin.

"You have his strong jaw," she sighed, her eyes glistening softly.

Maddy Rose knew her mother was remembering her father, who had fallen at the

Battle of Princeton last winter and lay with the others beneath the soil of New Jersey. Many men had gone to the war. Even her brother Jonathan, who was only fifteen, had joined Washington's army to wear the blue coat.

Outside, on the bustling streets, Maddy Rose marched along to the *rap tap tap* of tinsmiths, blacksmiths, and cobblers. She breathed in the mingled smells of sawdust, pitch, and baking bread as she passed cabinetmakers, coppersmiths, shipwrights, and bakers. She marveled at the swish of the weaver's shuttle, the blurred hands of busy lacemakers and seamstresses, hoping someday she would be as skilled.

From their busy shop fronts these hard-working folk traded with the wealthy loyalists, but out the back they gave what they could to the cause of freedom.

"Nothing's too good for them who soldier for our country," they all agreed.

Maddy Rose agreed too, for she was a Patriot rebel from head to toe in her homespun petticoats, her linsey-woolsey dress and muslin apron, her hand-me-down shoes, and woven straw hat. But it was her hand knit scarlet stockings that she valued the most, for their worth was far greater than just warm dry feet.

Whenever Maddy Rose strutted by the fine young ladies of Philadelphia in their creamy white stockings and dainty slippers, she'd raise her skirts and jut out her proud strong chin.

"Such poppycock!" she'd cluck to herself. No fancy silks, satins, and brocades imported from London for her. To wear such finery showed loyalty to the king.

Maddy Rose was loyal only to Jonathan. No one suspected her of anything, of course. Not this hardworking little seamstress who helped her poor mother by earning threepence. Why, she even hung the wash out every week like clockwork. But that's where Maddy Rose fooled them, for it was her small clothesline, hanging from her third-floor window, that held a secret code.

She'd lined her clothesline up perfectly with the harbor, just like when she and Jonathan used to play "Harbormaster." Jonathan pretended to be the harbormaster, cupping his hands like a spyglass, barking out docking and departing orders from an upper window. Maddy Rose scrambled below, playing the harbormaster's assistant, arranging cobblestones, apples, and scraps of wood as though they were real ships. Jonathan always tricked her so there would be a collision, then he'd make loud crashing and exploding sounds 'til they both laughed. It was only a game. But now things were different. The country was at war.

So once a week at dusk, using their secret code, Maddy Rose hung out her stockings and petticoats in the same order as the real ships along the wharf. A petticoat was code for a lightweight friendly vessel from the colonies. A scarlet stocking hanging toe up meant a merchant vessel from the islands or foreign port. When the toe hung down, it meant the vessel was suspicious and needed watching. But when the ship was riding low in the water, it meant only one thing–heavy firearms for the British. That's when Maddy Rose would weight that stocking down with a cobblestone.

Jonathan would sneak into the city after dark wearing a disguise, because if a spy were caught, he could be hanged. He'd read her clothesline then steal away through the darkened city to the countryside, relaying the information back to Washington's headquarters, so the Patriots were aware of who might be gunrunners and smugglers for the British. One time Jonathan disguised himself as a crippled beggar with a cane, limping badly. Maddy Rose became worried. But then he flipped into a perfect handstand, balancing on the cane like an acrobat. Oh how she laughed and clapped.

Once he saluted her like a puffed up rooster, then did an about-face, tripped on purpose, and fell flat as a flapjack, sending her into gales of laughter.

The last time he dressed as a woman, then hiked up his skirts and danced a wild jig in his long johns.

"Oh, Jonathan, you silly goat," Maddy Rose giggled from behind her window, then pulled in her clothesline and slept with a smile on her face.

Then, early one morn . . . **Ka-BOOM!**

The battle had started. British and Patriot cannons were blasting each other across Brandywine Creek. The ferocious bombardment was so loud that all of Philadelphia could hear it, even though it was twenty-five miles away. The date was September 11, 1777.

On that same foggy dawn, Jonathan hid in the mist with the Pennsylvania Line, lying low in the barleycorn fields and reedy banks along Brandywine Creek, clutching his musket as cannonballs screeched overhead, waiting for the command to attack the British redcoats on foot.

"Cannons!" Maddy Rose cried out as she tore downstairs. "Mother, do you not hear it?"

"Aye, child," she answered calmly, trying to spin as usual. "Be brave now. Let's get to work."

Maddy Rose tried not to think what those thundering cannons meant. She began pounding raspberry leaves as hard as she could. But the harder she pounded, the louder the cannons roared.

Ka-BOOM, BOOM!

She yanked the teakettle from the crane and spun around with the teacup in her hand. Just then . . .

KA-BOOM, BOOM . . . KA-BOOM!!

Maddy Rose jumped . . . and the precious teacup flew from her hand and smashed into a hundred bits and pieces.

The blazing cannons kept up their deadly attack, back and forth across Brandywine Creek 'til midday. Then came the command to charge, and the air became thick with the crack of muskets, the hiss of lead balls, and the awful smell of gunpowder smoke.

But Maddy Rose could not hear this part of the battle from where she sat in Ross's Upholstery Shop, ripping out seam after seam, unable to concentrate on the required sixteen stitches per inch.

"Maddy Rose, those seams can wait," said Mistress Ross kindly. She was a mild-mannered Quaker woman whose husband had fallen, too. "The *Tidewater*'s just docked from the Carolinas. Run down to the harbor and fetch my order of cotton batting and bindings."

"Yes, Ma'am," answered Maddy Rose eagerly. She needed to survey the harbor, for Jonathan would come soon after dark.

Maddy Rose's sharp eyes swept over the many ships crowded along the wharf. She memorized their positions, and which would be petticoats, which would be stockings with toes up, or toes down, but on this day she was startled to see that many stockings would need cobblestone weights.

Quickly she fetched Mistress Ross's order, but before she left, something made her look across the Delaware toward New Jersey, and her heart nearly stopped! For there, in the middle of the river, hiding among the many moored ships, sat a British man-of-war! "Jonathan must know this!" she gasped. Maddy Rose raced back and set to work. It was the heaviest clothesline she'd ever hung.

But that night Jonathan didn't come; yet Maddy Rose kept watch for him long into that black night. He didn't come the next night either, or the next, nor the one after that. More and more nights passed, yet she kept looking for him from her window, never losing hope.

Then, one night, a shadowy figure stood in Jonathan's place. She snuffed out her candle and peeked over the darkened sill. Who was he? Could it be Jonathan? But when he saw her window go dark he turned to leave.

Maddy Rose didn't even stop to think or slip on her shoes. She bounded after him, darting in and out of the shadows between the lampposts, stalking him like a silent cat in her stocking feet through the damp streets.

"Jonathan?" she whispered hopefully, shyly touching his cloak. "Is that you?"

The stranger turned and smiled. "I'm Seth," he answered. "And by the looks of your feet, you must be Little Miss Scarlet Stockings, Jonathan's sister."

"You know him? You know my brother?" she choked. Her face flushed hot and her throat tightened as she waited for Seth's answer.

But Seth was silent. Damp night air drifted in from the Delaware River, brushed against Maddy Rose's burning cheeks and seeped into Seth's eyes as he stared hard into the darkness. Then, solemnly, he bowed his head and spoke in a low voice.

"I'm proud to say I did, Miss."

Slowly Seth handed her a bundle. With trembling hands, she reached out, and for a few moments they held the bundle together.

Then Seth spoke softly. "I know your clothesline code, Miss," he said. "I've come to take Jonathan's place."

Maddy Rose nodded slowly as tears spilled from her eyes. She tried to hold up her chin, as her father would have, but it drooped as her bottom lip began to quiver.

"We'll not fail, Miss," Seth vowed. "I promise you that."

Then he was gone.

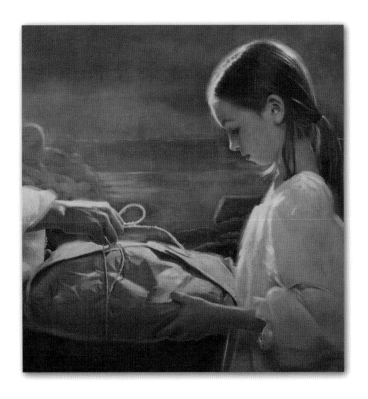

Back in her darkened room, Maddy Rose slowly untied the bundle. It was Jonathan's blue coat. Tenderly, she let her small fingers explore the blue wool serge until she found it—a stiff dried bloodstain. Then, with her littlest finger, she lightly traced two letters on the pewter buttons—U.S.

"Us," she whispered in the dark, ". . . for us, dear brother . . . for all of us."

That night, and for many nights to follow, Maddy Rose sat in her tiny room lit by a single candle, threaded her needle and sewed. She was making an American flag from her scarlet stockings, her white petticoats, and her brother's blue coat. And sewn into every one of her stitches was a tear of grief and the clenched fist of defiance.

Through the bleak cold winter that followed, Washington's army retreated to Valley Forge while the British occupied Philadelphia, lock, stock, and barrel. At night the redcoat invaders celebrated with military balls and fancy dances. And during the day they patrolled the streets, eyes forward, never noticing a young girl's stockings hanging overhead on a small clothesline from a third-floor window.

In the spring of 1778 the British left Philadelphia, crossed the Delaware, and were sent running by Washington's army at the Battle of Monmouth in New Jersey. The Patriots of Philadelphia celebrated, flying flags everywhere!

But there was one little flag that hung by itself on a small clothesline high over Appletree Alley. And fresh spring breezes traveled from New Jersey and found the little flag and lifted it up high. How proud and strong it flew, just like her father's chin, for it was Maddy Rose's

scarlet stockings flag.

Many years have passed since the spring of 1778. No one knows for sure what happened to this little flag. But if by chance you found it, in an old trunk or dusty attic or barn loft or musty museum basement, you would notice that one star is bigger than the rest. It sits in a place of honor, at the top of an arch of thirteen stars in a field of blue, the keystone star for Pennsylvania. And if you looked under that star, you would find a musket ball hole.

FROM THE AUTHOR,

Trinka Hakes Noble

The Scarlet Stockings Spy has deep personal meaning for me because my direct ancestor, James Hakes, was a soldier in the Revolutionary War. He traveled with his Connecticut regiment to Pennsylvania and New Jersey to join Washington's army from September 1776 to March 1777, where they distinguished themselves at the Battles of Trenton and Princeton. I set this story in the same time period.

American history has always been alive for me. Through my writing and storytelling, I am able to transport myself back to the times of my ancestors. In preparation for writing this story, I walked the battlefield at Princeton, New Jersey, retracing the footsteps of my ancestor who fought there more than 200 years ago. I was deeply moved and felt not only immense gratitude and pride, but a strong connection to those who came before me, to the characters in my story, to my own cherished freedom, and to my own country.

The Town that Fooled the British

THE WAR OF 1812

Lisa Papp

Illustrated by Robert Papp

Sometimes it doesn't take a giant to defeat one . . .

Click, clack, clack. The August air broke with the sound of shoes running wildly along the docks. Henry Middle's feet carried him fast, skidding around corners, kicking up the smooth Maryland dirt.

No, the day would not stay quiet.

"The British have captured the river!" Henry cried through the door of his father's shop.

That's the way the news came. It was summer 1813 and the people of St. Michaels' worst fears were coming true—a British attack.

Tucked along the banks of the Chesapeake Bay, this tiny river town had been well hidden.

But now the British saw St. Michaels as a threat.

St. Michaels was a town of shipbuilders. Eager and well-skilled, her citizens crafted some of the most valiant ships on the sea. It was their own Baltimore Clippers and other powerful schooners that struck fear in the mighty British Navy.

Weary of their losses at sea, even the British newspapers were calling for destruction of the American towns that made the great warships.

St. Michaels could no longer hide from the war.

For weeks, the British had been snaking their way up the Chesapeake Bay, attacking villages and burning towns. And now it was clear they had chosen their next target.

Henry struggled to catch his breath. "I saw the scouts riding in. I overheard what they said! Is it true—are the British really coming?"

Even before his father could answer, Henry saw gunpowder and a musket on the table. Henry's father served in the town's militia.

"I fear it is true," he said, pulling on his uniform jacket. A loose button spun to the floor and Henry picked it up.

"What can I do?" Henry said, slipping the button into his pocket.

"Not now, my son. There will be meetings, so I must hurry." Still wanting to help, Henry reached for his father's canteen. But his father spoke first. "Evacuations will begin soon, Henry. I want you home with your mother and sister."

"But I . . ." Henry began, then seeing his father's face, said no more. Henry stepped out of the shop, wishing he could do more.

The news spread quickly through town. When Henry arrived home, his mother and sister were already in the garden. "We'll harvest what we can," his mother said, "for when they come, we may lose everything."

Henry imagined British soldiers picking through their garden, taking what they pleased. He refused to think about what could happen to his house and to the room he had always shared with his sister. Beneath the darkening skies, some of Henry's fear was replaced with anger.

Henry's mother folded the last of her herbs into a linen cloth while his sister clung to her doll. "We'll not be joining the evacuation," she said. Henry's mother was skilled in nursing and wanted to be available if needed. "Our cellar is well hidden; we'll be safe below."

Henry watched his mother lift two lanterns from the tiny nook beneath the window. " 'Tis a shame," she said. "Your father will have greater need for these than we will."

"Let me!" Henry pleaded, still wanting to help. "I can find Father—I can bring him the lanterns." Without waiting for an answer, Henry tucked the lanterns beneath his arms and raced for the door.

"Wait!" his mother called.

Henry froze. "I want to do something."

His mother placed her hands on his thin shoulders. Then, she looked into his eyes and understood. "Quickly, my child. Make haste!"

Henry dashed into the street and gasped.

The evacuation had begun. Families, carrying what they could, crowded the village streets, driven by a new sense of urgency. Those unable to walk were carried in carts while livestock clamored alongside.

Henry quickened his pace. *I have to find Father*, he thought again and again.

When Henry arrived, St. Mary's Square was swarming with soldiers. Militia marched in lines while scouts raced by on horseback.

Clutching his lanterns, he searched for his father, but in the sea of uniforms everyone looked the same.

Above the bustling square, a strong wind brought heavy clouds and Henry felt the start of rain.

A unit of men hurried past, talking nervously of cannons and ships and British soldiers clad in red. Not a one seemed to know the hour the British would come. Only that they were coming.

"There will be cannons, no doubt, and gunmen coming ashore," said a man Henry had not seen before. "They will be well trained and dangerous." The voice belonged to General Perry Benson, who had fought boldly in the Revolutionary War.

"We are ready to fight," answered a soldier, "but what are men against cannons?"

Henry shuddered; a part of him wished he were home with his mother. Now soaking wet, his tears mixed easily with the falling rain and he almost didn't know he was crying.

Henry clutched the lanterns tightly. One face blended into another. He scanned the crowd again. Where was his father?

Deep within the mist, the British celebrated their luck! For this storm created the perfect cover for their lurking ships. Their time had finally come to destroy the renowned Maryland shipbuilders.

C ... R ... E ... A ... K ... the British ships leaned and felt their way through the clouded Chesapeake waters.

At St. Mary's Square, evening drew close and with it the dread of what was coming. The constant talk of cannons filled the air. Henry's heart raced, beating faster than the pouring rain. With the lanterns pressed tightly against his chest he suddenly remembered his mother's words ... *Your father will have greater need for these ...*

"The lanterns!" Henry shouted.

Still searching for his father, Henry saw a buttonless sleeve sweep past.

"Father!" Henry said against the rain. "The lanterns—we can hang them in the trees." There was no response. Reaching for his father's arm Henry stumbled and found himself face to face with the general instead.

General Benson leaned forward, the water pouring from the brim of his hat. "What did you say?"

"The lanterns," Henry said. "We can hang them in the trees."

Henry's father, stirred by his son's voice, pushed his way through the crowd.

"Sorry, sir," Henry's father said. "I didn't know he was here, I'll . . . "

But the general's eyes remained on Henry.

Slowly he began to smile. "Gather all the lanterns!" he commanded his men. "Search the town, find every last one."

Into the branches of trees they climbed and onto the masts of ships, upon every high place, the lanterns were hung.

Throughout the night, the message was sent: put out all the town's remaining lights!

Henry reached for one more lantern but his father shook his head, "Your mother needs you now. Go." Henry nodded; then,

taking one last look at the lanterns, raced for home.

And so it was, in the predawn of August 10, 1813, amid heavy fog and driving rain, the British arrived at St. Michaels.

Aboard the British brig, cannons lined the ship. Soldiers stood ready, eager for battle.

"Find your marks! . . . *Fire!*"

The cannons roared, one after the other, chasing the lights of the tiny town, thundering across the water.

BOOM . . . boom **BOOM!** Gunpowder scorched the air. Metal wheels ground against wood as the cannons were packed and reloaded.

The bombardment continued without rest, for the British were well stocked.

The cellar offered little comfort as the deafening sound of cannons splintered the air. Henry rolled the button over and over in his hand. All he could do now was wait.

With each new wave of attack, his stomach churned with uncertainty.

"Are they getting closer?" his sister asked. "Where is Father, is he safe?"

"Shhh, my child," was all his mother would say.

Finally, before the breaking dawn, it stopped. All became still.

As the first bit of sunlight spread across the skies, Henry crept to the door and dared to look out. A broad figure moved toward him. Henry recognized the familiar walk and at last his father's face came into view. He held a broken lantern in one hand.

"Father!" Henry cried, running toward him.

Soon he was wrapped in his father's arms. "It worked," his father whispered.

With nothing to aim at but the dim lights hung high in the trees, the British overshot the town entirely. St. Michaels was safe; not a single home or ship was lost in the battle. Still cloaked by fog, the British ships sneaked away, assuming victory.

Henry's father loosened his grip. "Henry," he said, looking proudly into his son's eyes, "sometimes it doesn't take a giant to defeat one."

FROM THE AUTHOR,
Lisa Papp

Today, St. Michaels is a gently bustling tourist town. The streets are laid out exactly as they were in 1813, and if you walk the narrow lanes by the harbor, you can imagine what life was like for a small boy during a time when America was learning that becoming a nation held its own growing pains.

Although Henry Middle is a fictional character, the events surrounding the defense of his town are real. General Perry Benson, who fought with George Washington in the War for Independence just 30 years prior, played a key role in defending the town.

In telling this small part of a larger story, I hope to spark an interest in a much-overlooked part of our country's heroic beginnings. This was a war that gave birth to our "Star Spangled Banner," the icon Uncle Sam and, many believe, gave the White House its popular name.

—∿—

In memory of James C. Dugent,
Captain Commanding
"Baltimore United Volunteers."
Thank you for bringing history to life.

—*Robert and Lisa Papp*

The
Last Brother

THE CIVIL WAR

Trinka Hakes Noble
Illustrated by Robert Papp

On the morning of July 1, 1863, the peaceful little town of Gettysburg awoke, early as usual. Front porches were swept clean, feather beds aired, and blackberry jam bubbled on the stove. In the town square, old men dozed in the shade while small barefoot boys scampered toward Seminary Ridge carrying fishing poles and berry pails.

One mile across from Seminary Ridge rose Cemetery Ridge flanked by Little Round Top and Big Round Top to the south and Cemetery and Culp's Hill to the north. In the rich valley below, tidy farms and fields spread out like a patchwork quilt stitched together with split rail fences.

Yet the Civil War had raged for two years. Gettysburg was only seven miles from the Mason-Dixon Line. When rumors reached the old men that Confederate troops had pushed north into Pennsylvania, they kept a watchful lookout for signs of war. But the barefoot boys up on Seminary Ridge saw it first . . . two massive clouds of dust gathering on either horizon as two armies moved closer.

In one cloud of dust marched a young boy in a blue uniform, with a full knapsack, a canteen, and a brass bugle slung over his shoulder. His name was Gabriel and he was a bugler in the Union Army, even though he was only eleven.

Gabe was the youngest in a big Pennsylvania farm family of four boys and five girls. He'd run away with his brother Davy, who was sixteen, to join up. When the recruiting officer asked Davy his age, Davy honestly replied, "I'm over eighteen" because he had slipped a piece of paper inside his shoe with 18 penciled on it.

Then he pointed at Gabe. "Think you can blow a bugle for the Keystone State, boy?"

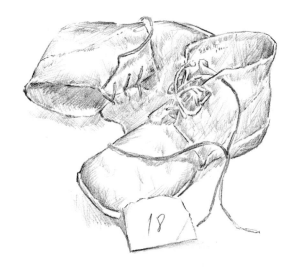

Gabriel nodded, "I can learn, sir."

Lots of boys Davy's age got the war fever, longing for adventure and glory. But Gabe had his own reason for tagging after Davy.

Joshua and Tucker, Gabe's two oldest brothers, had marched off to join the Union Army when President Lincoln first called for volunteers after the firing on Fort Sumter in 1861.

"It's just for ninety days," Josh and Tuck assured their ma and pa. "Come harvest-time, we'll be back. Can't expect these two little runts to handle it," they joked, playfully pushing Davy and Gabe.

But Ma and Pa looked serious. "You are the sons of old Pennsylvania now," they said.

How proudly Josh and Tuck marched off in their blue uniforms. Davy and Gabe

had raced alongside, shouting "the Union forever!" while their sisters cheered, waving white handkerchiefs.

But harvesttime came and went. Ninety days stretched into a year, then two, until finally, one day, the sad news came and those ninety days had become forever. That's when Gabe knew Davy would enlist and he would follow.

So now Gabe and Davy were the boys in blue. Gabe pulled his cap low and squinted. He searched for Davy marching with the 71st Pennsylvania, but the dust was too thick. So many regiments and brigades had joined the long blue column, with flags flying from every northern state from Maine to Michigan to Minnesota. Gabe had never seen so many soldiers.

"Keep up, boy!" ordered a sergeant. "No stragglers! We got a full day's march to Gettysburg."

"Yes, sir," Gabe obeyed and quickstepped forward, keeping his eye on Lancer up ahead, the major's powerful chestnut horse.

"Keep up, boy!" ordered a sergeant. "No stragglers! We got a full day's march to Gettysburg."

"Yes, sir," Gabe obeyed and quickstepped forward, keeping his eye on Lancer up ahead, the major's powerful chestnut horse.

Lancer was a trained military horse, with the letters U.S. branded on his hindquarter. Neither busting shells nor flying bullets spooked him. He'd charge into battle, knowing all the commands almost before they were called.

Like Lancer, Gabe knew all the commands, too. There were over 60 different battle calls for young buglers to learn. The problem in the Civil War was that the Confederate Army had the same calls. So it was crucial for troops to learn the style of their own bugler, especially in battle. So Gabriel practiced long and hard. And to make sure his regiment knew it was him, he put a little uplifting lilt in each call. But unlike Lancer, Gabe had never been in a real battle.

The next day they made camp below Cemetery Ridge. Already fighting and clashes had broken out. Cannon smoke hung heavy in the air. Up on Cemetery Hill Gabe could see dozens of artillery batteries pointed toward the enemy.

Immediately, the major called for scouts and Davy was the first to step forward. Gabe nervously watched his brother vanish into the smoke while Army mules rumbled by hauling more cannons and heavy wagons loaded with grapeshot and canister shells.

Gabe knew he wouldn't be needed right away, so he slipped into the densely wooded hillsides and sat by a stream to practice battle calls. He stuffed his handkerchief in his bugle's bell and softly blew "commence fire." To his surprise, a bugle softly answered from across the stream with "cease fire." Gabe looked but saw no one, so he blew "fix bayonets" and instantly heard "unfix bayonets." Astounded, Gabe stood and blew a full "charge" and back came "retreat"!

Suddenly a boy peeked out from the bushes with a bugle in one hand, a fishing pole in the other, and a big old grin on his dirty freckled face. He splashed across the stream to Gabe.

"Howdy! I'm Orlee. You sure know how to blow that horn."

"I'm Gabriel," Gabe smiled, happy to meet a boy his own age.

Orlee started gabbing like they were old friends. "Gabriel . . . now that's a right fancy name. My paw wanted to give me a fancy name but Maw wanted to call me Lee. Paw kept thinkin' up fancier and fancier names like Beauregard and Bertram, but Maw kept saying 'or Lee.' She had to say it so many times that pretty soon they just called me Orlee."

Gabe laughed and Orlee chuckled. It'd been a long time since either boy had laughed.

"Bet'cha thought I was named after General Robert E. Lee, didn't ya?" Orlee winked. "Nah, not in the Mississippi hills I growed up in. Maw figured a name like Lee with just three letters, 'specially with two of them the same, would be real easy for a feller to keep track of. A right smart woman, my maw."

Then Orlee paused and quietly asked, "Do your home folks call you Gabe?"

Gabe nodded silently and for a moment both boys tried to remember the sound of their mothers' voices. That's when Gabe noticed Orlee had scratched his name and regiment, the 11th Mississippi, on the bell of his bugle, just in case.

But Orlee wasn't silent for long. "I was sneakin' in a little fishin'," he teased, "and you come by and blew 'commence fire' and those fish skedaddled faster than fat hens on market day!"

"Bet they're hiding right under that fallen log," Gabe grinned, remembering the best place to catch brook trout back home was under the covered bridge.

So the two boys sat down to fish. Soon Orlee asked, "Got anything to trade?" Gabe swapped some army hardtack for a bit of Orlee's fatback. Then Orlee handed Gabe some Virginia pipe tobacco and said, "Don't smoke it. It's like gold. You can trade tobacco for anything." So Gabe gave Orlee his ration of coffee and they divided the fish.

As they departed, the two young buglers
played taps to each other as a way of saying
farewell. Gabe couldn't help but notice a
sad downturn in his friend's bugle call and
it worried him.

But, for a short time, the old hills of Pennsylvania shielded the northern boy and the southern lad from what was to come.

When Gabe got back to camp, Davy hadn't returned. But there were other duties for a bugle boy to perform. So Gabe carried firewood, filled canteens, and watered the major's horse.

While Lancer drank, Gabe leaned into his side and lightly traced a long, jagged scar across the horse's broad chest. "Lancer," he whispered, "I wish you could tell me what it's like to be in battle."

When Gabe thought about Josh and Tuck, he wanted to cry. Now Davy was in the fight. What if Davy didn't come back like Josh and Tuck? For a moment, Gabe buried his face in Lancer's mane as the great horse gently wrapped his powerful neck and head around the boy.

Suddenly, Lancer whinnied low. Gabe jerked around. There stood Orlee, solemn, in full uniform, his finger pressed against his lips.

"Gabe," he whispered seriously. "We got battle orders. My whole regiment's assembled just yonder." Then he silently waved the back of his hand at Gabe. "Best hightail it out of here with that horse before they see you."

Gabe grabbed Lancer's reins, shot a nervous glance toward the clearing, and silently mouthed the words "thank you" as he pulled Lancer around.

"Gabe," Orlee softly called after him, "if you ever git to Mississippi someday . . . "

Gabe nodded over his shoulder, "God willing, we'll fish again if . . . " but Orlee had already vanished. Gabe hurried Lancer out of sight.

It was long after dark before Davy returned, exhausted, his face streaked with gunpowder and sweat. He wolfed down the fish stew Gabe had saved for him, drained a fresh canteen, and sprawled on the ground until he caught his breath.

"We fought the Rebs in the woods today," he said hoarsely, his eyes closed. "Gabe, some of them aren't any older than me." Gabe nodded, but didn't tell Davy about Orlee.

"The Confederates are all over that far ridge, down near Little Round Top, too," Davy reported. "They captured the town. Got sharpshooters in the church towers. Folks are hiding in their cellars. Almost took Culp's Hill. Gabe, we're nearly out-flanked. See those campfires along Cemetery Ridge? Well, some of them are fake, kept going by a couple picket guards, trying to fool the Confederates into thinking we've got more men."

Davy stood, anxious to clean and reload his rifle, then paused. "Get some sleep, little brother. We'll see heavy action tomorrow." Gabe could see the burning embers reflected in Davy's eyes. "Gabe," he said slowly, "all the Pennsylvania boys volunteered to go first, so stay on the safe side of the major's horse tomorrow." Then he was gone.

All through the night the Union campfires burned on Cemetery Ridge, but Gabe couldn't sleep. He kept thinking about Davy and Orlee, afraid of what might happen tomorrow. When he peeked from his bedroll, the flickering firelight cast ominous shadows of troops digging defensive earthworks, mules hauling heavy supply wagons, and more soldiers creeping in under the cover of darkness.

At dawn, the campfires blinked out, one by one. When Gabe sounded reveille for his regiment, scores of other regimental buglers echoed up and down the ridge. There, concealed just below Cemetery Ridge, was the whole Union Army—entrenched, ready and waiting.

That morning Gabe's regiment could hear heavy gunfire as they marched into position on the north section of Cemetery Ridge behind the gunners. Gabe stood next to

Lancer, at his post, bugle in hand. Davy waited in the front line, his rifle loaded, at the ready.

Then, at midday, from across the valley, Confederate cannons opened fire and Union cannons roared back with a thundering blast that shook the earth. Shells exploded everywhere. The deafening blast knocked Gabe off balance. He grabbed onto Lancer.

"Hold steady, boys!" shouted the major. "They can't dislodge the Old Keystone!"

The Union artillery gunners were relentless, firing volley after volley. Gunpowder smoke burned Gabe's eyes, choked his throat, and scorched his lungs. The Confederate cannons stubbornly pounded back, ripping into the Union lines. With each blast, blinding dirt, sizzling shell fragments, and lead grapeshot hissed through the ranks. The massive bombardment kept up, nonstop, from both sides for two deadly hours. But the Keystone held.

When the thick smoke cleared, Gabe stiffened with fear at what he saw. For there, pouring out from behind the trees on Seminary Ridge, were thousands upon thousands of Confederate troops, advancing across the valley. What had once been a patchwork quilt of tidy farms and fields was now a swarming mass of soldiers in gray, charging toward the Union lines. Chills shot up Gabe's spine. Lancer's head jerked violently, his ears flattened.

"*Forward!*" ordered the major as the first bullets whizzed overhead. Somehow Gabe blew "forward" and the 71st Infantry moved in front of the field guns and cannons like a precision machine and took cover behind a stone wall.

"Ready on the firing line! *Commence fire!*" Gabe could barely breathe but sounded the command and a storm of bullets smashed into the Confederate lines.

"Fire at will! Fire at will! Fire at will!" was shouted up and down the Union lines. Gabe shook, yet stayed on his feet. Blood streamed down Lancer's leg. Davy blurred into a solid fortress of blue, firing and reloading, firing and reloading, firing and reloading. But still the Confederates kept coming, firing back, determined to break the Union lines. The gunfire from both sides was so intense, so thick, that some Union and Confederate bullets actually crashed into each other in midair and fell to the ground. But many hit their mark, until both sides had nearly exhausted their ammo.

Then, the major drew his sword, pointed it skyward and yelled, "For Pennsylvania and the Union–*Charge!!*"

Lancer lunged forward . . . but Gabe hesitated.

For an instant, Gabe wanted to sound "re-treat," to save Davy fighting in the front lines. But there was Orlee, somewhere on the other side. Again, the major commanded ***"Charge! Charge!!"*** but no sound came from the boy. What could he do?

Suddenly, Gabe knew what to do. He forced a deep gulp of air and blew "charge" as fast as he could. Then, unnoticed in the confusion of battle, he ran onto the battlefield and instantly blew "retreat," copying Orlee's style. And for a brief moment, the firing stopped.

In this deadliest of battles, later known as Pickett's Charge, with thousands of casualties in just fifty minutes, there was only one small section of the battle line where not a single life was lost on either side.

At dusk on that final day of the bloodiest battle in American history, a young bugler climbed to the top of Cemetery Hill. He stood on a wagon to make himself taller, for he was only eleven. He faced west across the valley, raised his bugle to his lips, and played taps.

The bittersweet refrain seemed to rise up from the boy's very soul and join in harmony with the softening twilight. Both gray and blue caps were removed and held over hearts. The shell-shocked folks of Gettysburg emerged from their cellars and, for a moment, the pain of the wounded was eased. And, far out on the battlefield, one injured horse rose to his feet and slowly limped toward the sound.

The boy held the last note for a very long time, so long that it seemed to reach eternity.

Then, faintly, from far across the valley, a

bugler answered with a sad downturn that echoed through the darkening hills. The boy in blue drew to attention, lowered his bugle, and saluted. The Battle of Gettysburg was over.

All through that long night, the young bugler tenderly cared for his wounded brother and the injured horse. And when the first pale pink blush of dawn crept into the eastern sky, he sat by the campfire next to his brother and etched these words on his bugle . . .

For all my brothers, on this day and forever . . .

It was July 4, 1863.

FROM THE AUTHOR,
Trinka Hakes Noble

The Civil War is sometimes called the boys' war because those who served were so young. Many drummers and buglers were between the ages of ten and fourteen. It wasn't until I walked the battlefield at Gettysburg that I began to realize the depth and enormity of what happened there. The culmination of this three-day battle at Pickett's Charge seemed beyond reason, yet soldiers did survive in pockets up and down the three-mile-long battle line. The highly emotional content of this story was drawn from that experience.

The Last Brother was written with deep respect and honor, not only for my ancestors, but for all who served in the Civil War.

Trinka Hakes Noble is the author of numerous children's books such as *The Orange Shoes* and *The People of Twelve Thousand Winters*. Her many awards include ALA Notable Children's Book, *Booklist* Children's Editors' Choice, IRA-CBC Children's Choice, *Learning*: The Year's Ten Best, and several Junior Literary Guild selections. Ms. Noble lives in northern New Jersey.

Lisa Papp attended Iowa State University College of Design and studied three more years at duCret School of Art, where she won numerous awards. Her illustration work includes *One for All: A Pennsylvania Number Book* and Eve Bunting's *My Mom's Wedding*. *The Town that Fooled the British* marked her writing debut.

Robert Papp formally trained at duCret School of Art. His award-winning artwork includes hundreds of illustrations for major publishers across the United States. Previous children's books include *M is for Meow: A Cat Alphabet* and *P is for Princess: A Royal Alphabet*, which he and Lisa illustrated together. Rob and Lisa live in historic Bucks County, Pennsylvania.